CHIP RICHARDS

FLUTES IN THE GARDEN

Illustrated by O.B. De Alessi

BLUE ANGEL®
PUBLISHING

FLUTES IN THE GARDEN

Published by Blue Angel Publishing®
80 Glen Tower Drive, Glen Waverley
Victoria, Australia 3150
Email: info@blueangelonline.com
Website: www.blueangelonline.com

Edited by Tanya Graham

Illustrated by O.B. De Alessi

Blue Angel is a registered trademark of Blue Angel Gallery Pty. Ltd.

ISBN: 978-1-922161-36-9

For Joshua and Asheyana,
my two greatest teachers of magic and miracles in life.

Both of you are truly both of these to me.

There was a farmer who lived
with his wife and son
in a great and fertile land.

For more information on this
or any Blue Angel Publishing® release,
please visit our website at:

www.blueangelonline.com

About the Author

An internationally published author, speaker and creative guide, Chip Richard's writing career spans the mediums of feature film, fiction, poetry and journalism. With an honors degree in English from Dartmouth College, Chip made his mainstream screenwriting debut as the writer of the critically acclaimed feature film, *One Perfect Day*. As a consultant and creative guide, Chip works internationally with business leaders and organisations to help craft a 'new story' for our planet through meaningful work in the world. Chip has shared his vision for "Becoming the Hero of Your Own Life Story" on stages from Google to TEDx, and he is a host of the global festival and online media channel, UPLIFT (www.upliftconnect.com). His love of story and passion for igniting the creative gifts of others has propelled him to create the *Writing the Story Within* experience (book, CD, DVD and mentorship program) as a pathway for individuals of all walks to bring their creative visions through onto the page... and out to the world. He is also the author of *The Secret Language of Animals* and *Animal Voices* oracle deck series. Chip lives in the hinterland of Northern New South Wales, Australia, immersed in the beauty of his family, their animals, the ocean and their garden.

About the Artist

O.B. De Alessi is an Italian artist working between Paris, London and Italy and currently living in Paris. She graduated from Chelsea College of Art and Design in London and from Accademia Di Belle Arti in Bologna. She has had both solo and group exhibitions in Europe as well as South America, Australia and Russia. Her work has been published in numerous books and magazines. Visit her website at www.obdealessi.com

The TRUTH about Plants and Music!

In some special scientific places around the world, it is also quite
commonly accepted that plants – as living beings – respond
to our thoughts, words, visions…and also to our songs. Many
experiments have been done where plants of all types have grown
faster, bigger and more fruitful when listening to classical and
harmonious music. Unfortunately they grow a bit slower when
they listen to hard rock-and-roll, so for now, it may be best to
stick with your flute, harp, guitar or sweetest singing voice when
playing in the garden… Step into your garden today…and play!

The TRUTH about Tiny Gardeners!

In certain special places around the world it is quite commonly accepted and expected that 'nature spirits' and 'devas' oversee the growth and vitality of all plants and flowers. It is speculated that every single plant and every blade of grass has its own unique spirit to care for and protect it. These little beings are known to be quite helpful and co-operative with those who lovingly create gardens, homes and special experiences in nature. If you knew this were true…how would you approach your garden today?

THE END

… And Friday nights, when the farmer, and his family opened their porch as a café, so all who wished could come and eat fresh food grown on their land, while listening to family farm music… and the growing sound of flutes in the garden.

… And Tuesday nights, when he ran a class for other farmers
who wanted to discover the secret symphony hidden
in their garden crops…

From that day forward, the farmer was able to go back to sleeping a few more hours each night, while the tiny gardeners played their flutes and tended the garden. Except for Sunday nights, when his presence was required to teach a new song…

When the Purest of Dreams
Meets the Purest of Songs,
The Purest of Life Will Always
Spring Forth.
By Playing the Notes of Your
Heart—With Flute or Voice or
Stomping Feet—You Open the
Way for the World to Do
THE SAME!

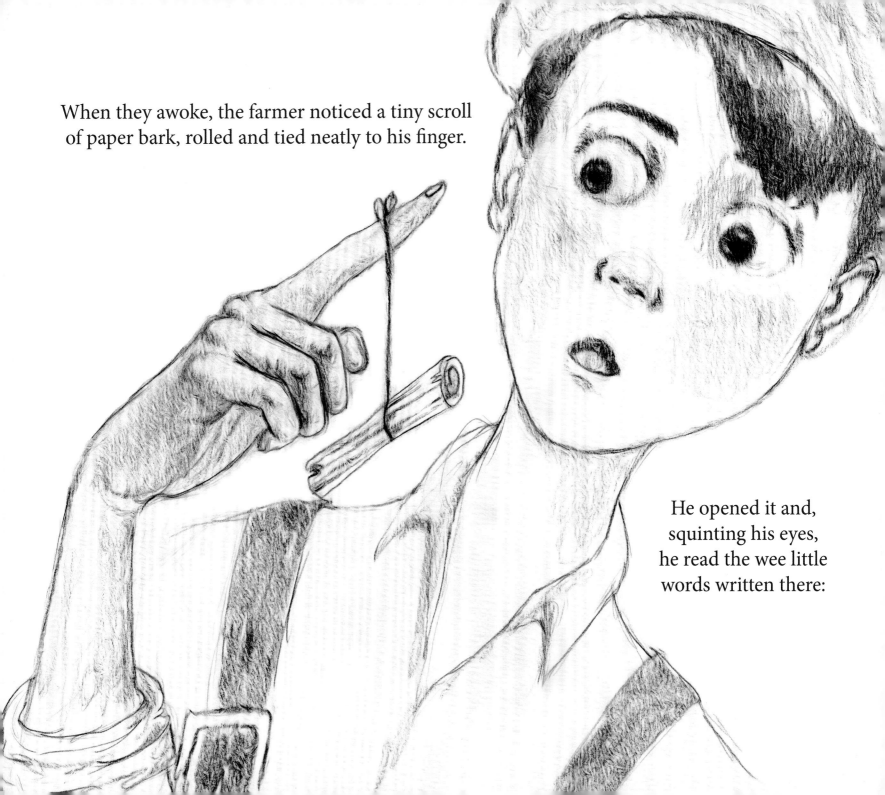

When they awoke, the farmer noticed a tiny scroll of paper bark, rolled and tied neatly to his finger.

He opened it and, squinting his eyes, he read the wee little words written there:

Eventually, near the new dawn, as the clouds cleared and the sun prepared to rise, the farmer, his wife and their sweet son fell fast asleep together on the porch swing.

As players kept playing and workers moved through their tasks, the farmer slowly quieted his own flute playing and his wife and son followed suit until they all stood quietly in the moonlight, watching the miniature symphony of music and garden growth unfold into the night. They were filled with gratitude.

And then the most extraordinary thing happened…
Something that hadn't happened for many months…

It began to rain.

First little drops…

Then big ones, splashing down from the night sky, across all the lands in the shire. The rain brought new celebration and zest to the gardeners, spurring them joyfully on in their tasks.

Fireflies darted through the air and the breeze whistled through lettuce leaves, all in time with the growing rhythm of working, dancing and playing in the garden. The farmer's son began stomping to the beat and his wife could not help joining the tiny garden chorus with her own voice from the porch.

As the little band began to taste their treats, smiles emerged across their normally focused faces. Then another among them opened the second box… There inside was a stack of teeny, tiny flutes, intricately crafted from the tips of bamboo branches.

The miniature flutes were passed out to several of the tiny gardeners who, one-by-one, cautiously began to play. At first they were a little awkward, but soon an ensemble formed at the base of a zucchini vine and began playing right along with the farmer! Young ones started to dance, and a few tiny women gardeners began to open their voices and sing!

As usual, the farmer began to play his flute, and his family watched on as the little band emerged just like they had many nights before.

When they reached the centre of the garden and saw the little wooden boxes, they all stopped and looked around. Cautiously, one of the elders among them approached and opened the first box. Inside was a batch of miniature mulberry pies, made entirely from ingredients found in the garden (ground cornmeal, berries and a few drops of dew from agave flowers).

That evening,
just after the sunset,
the three of them snuck
into the garden and placed two
little wooden chests in a little
clearing just past the strawberries.

The only problem was that the farmer was exhausted!!

Besides an occasional afternoon nap, he'd only had one full night of sleep the whole month (on that night, he played a recording of his flute through the stereo, but the results were not quite the same).

Then one day, the farmer's son had an idea… It seemed a bit far-fetched at first, but they figured it was worth a try.

So the farmer and his son spent the day in the shed, sawing and drilling, while the farmer's wife spent her day in the kitchen cutting and cooking.

By the end of the month the farmer and his family had
filled their cans of savings, and given a lot of extra food to
friends and neighbours… and along the way they
had developed a real sense of kinship with this group of
tiny gardeners who they never previously knew existed.

For the next week, the farmer stayed up every night
playing his flute and in the morning his garden was full.
Off to the market he would go, and in the afternoon,
he and his son would clear more space and plant new
seeds. By the following morning, whatever they planted –
from pumpkins to string beans – would be ripe!

It was late and the farmer hadn't slept all week,
but barely did he blink the rest of the night, for there
amidst the working rhythms of this little band of
gardeners, the plants of his garden began to sprout,
blossom and fruit right before his eyes!

On through the night this continued, until the glow
of sunrise peaked into the valley, and the first call of
kookaburra echoed in the trees. As the farmer brought
his song to quiet completion, the little team of gardeners
slipped back into the underbrush... and disappeared.

They moved with great lightness and speed
– balancing, bounding and swinging through
the leaves as they worked – all in time with
the melody of the farmer's flute!

They even had tiny bamboo-shoot hoses,
pumping water from the roots of the mulberry tree!

A crew of tiny little elf-like people… men, women and youngsters, moving quietly through the garden. They had rakes made of fairy wren feathers and shovels made of twigs and shells…

That night, after lighting the candle, and saying his prayer, the farmer climbed back up into the mulberry tree, this time with binoculars, tea, blanket… and his flute. He waited for the animals and insects to go to sleep, and in that magic window of silent time… he began to quietly play.

As the flute song trickled into the night, the farmer began to notice gentle movements throughout the garden, right down near the ground. He stopped playing and instantly the movement stopped.

What was it? A rabbit? A lizard? A snake?

Cautiously, the farmer continued to play, and again the garden began to move… the pumpkins were bobbing, the celery swaying and the leaves of silverbeet were all gently waving in the air – in time with his flute!

The farmer leaned forward, peering into the binoculars. There, to his great surprise, he saw…

Afraid that he had scared off whatever good fortune had found him, the farmer shared exactly what had happened with his wife and little boy. They too were mystified, but after a moment his son pointed out the one key ingredient that was missing from the previous night in the garden…

His dad's flute.

The farmer did not believe that his simple playing could have such an influence on the garden's growth, but after much insisting by his family, he agreed to stay up one more night and try again, this time playing his flute.

When the sun rose in the morning,
the farmer leapt down from the tree with great
expectation, but was disappointed to find no
new growth at all in the garden.

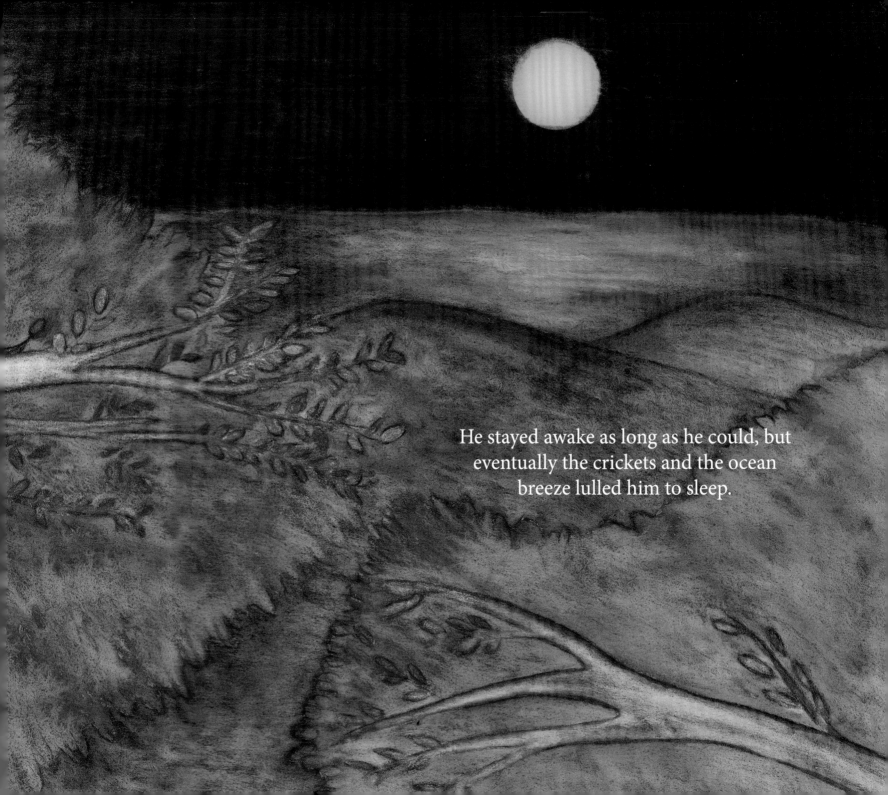

He stayed awake as long as he could, but eventually the crickets and the ocean breeze lulled him to sleep.

That night, after another successful day at the market,
and another beautiful evening meal with his family, the
farmer was determined to discover what was really going
on. So he brewed a thermos full of tea, lit his prayerful
candle and climbed up into the mulberry tree with
binoculars, ready to keep watch for the night...

The following morning he woke to discover another burst of amazing growth in the garden! Even more than the day before! As the farmer eagerly picked the vegetables, he couldn't help noticing that the soil around them was neatly raked, weeded and damp to the touch... as though it had been watered and cared for in the night. Even the leaves and fruit seemed to shimmer as though they had been polished. It was as if someone had been in the garden working the soil and tending to the plants in the night. How could this be? *Who* could this be?

The farmer quickly woke his family to be sure he wasn't dreaming, and together, with surprised joy, they harvested the crop and loaded the truck for market.

The farmer's fruit and veggies were so ripe and colourful that he sold every single item in the truck.

That night, after sharing a fresh meal with his family (including a mulberry pie), the farmer settled back onto the porch, lit another candle, said another prayer and once again played his flute to the garden.

He played even longer into the night eventually drifting off to sleep again.

A few hours later, the farmer woke to the first
beams of sunrise, and a most amazing sight.
The patch of garden just next to the porch had
somehow completely blossomed overnight.
It was full of fresh, ripe fruit and vegetables!

The tomatoes were glowing red and full of juice,
the cucumbers were huge and emerald green,
even the carrots had pushed their way down
through the dry soil, radiant and orange.

The farmer played his flute into
the night until he had played
himself to sleep, right there in
the porch swing.

And in his playing he began to dream of a
garden ripe and overflowing…

He dreamed of food growing so
abundantly that there was more than enough
to share. He dreamed of vines overflowing with
fruit and baskets piled high at the markets.
He dreamed of laughter and ease, wellness
and joy for all.

He played to
the audience of
stars, crickets and
fireflies.

He played into the
silence of the sky
beyond.

He played into the
cracks of the dry
and thirsty soil.

He played to the
creatures of the
night.

As he sat down on the porch swing, he noticed his
flute sitting in the corner, covered in cobwebs with the
beginnings of a wasp nest at one end. He hadn't played
his flute in months, and indeed it hardly seemed the right
time. Yet strangely, he found himself reaching through
the dusty webs to pick it up.

He gently cleaned it off, closed his eyes and began to play.
Cautiously at first, but soon a song came through and
found him, and seemed to carry him into the night.

So he lit a candle,
and said a prayer as he looked out
across his barren land.

On the evening of his very last harvest, the farmer kissed his wife and son
to sleep and went out to the porch to think about what to do. He knew in
his heart that there must be an answer, but with nothing left in the garden
to take to market, he did not know what that answer could be…

But as the years went on and life grew all around them, the farmer found there was less and less time to play his flute. His wife sung fewer songs and they spoke little of their dreams, and more of the bills that needed paying and jobs that needed doing…

One year, there came no rain for many months. Creeks ran dry and water tanks emptied. The farmer's crops began to suffer. There was barely enough water for them to drink, let alone for the garden. The farmer knew that without some positive shift of good fortune, the garden – and all they had worked for – would be lost.

After dinner, he would sit out on the porch and play a song or two on his flute – sometimes joined by the beautiful voice of his wife.

They would imagine that the fireflies were torches of a great audience and the crickets were a chorus of applause. It felt good.

They sometimes dreamed of opening a café on their farm, where people could enjoy fresh baked meals from their garden while listening to live music as they ate.

In the evening he would come home to his
family, eat fresh food from the garden
(including fresh mulberry pie when in season)
and play with his son.

He spent most mornings tilling the soil,
planting seeds and harvesting fruits and vegetables.

He spent most afternoons loading his harvest into his
truck and driving into town where he sold his crops
at the village market, restaurants and shops.